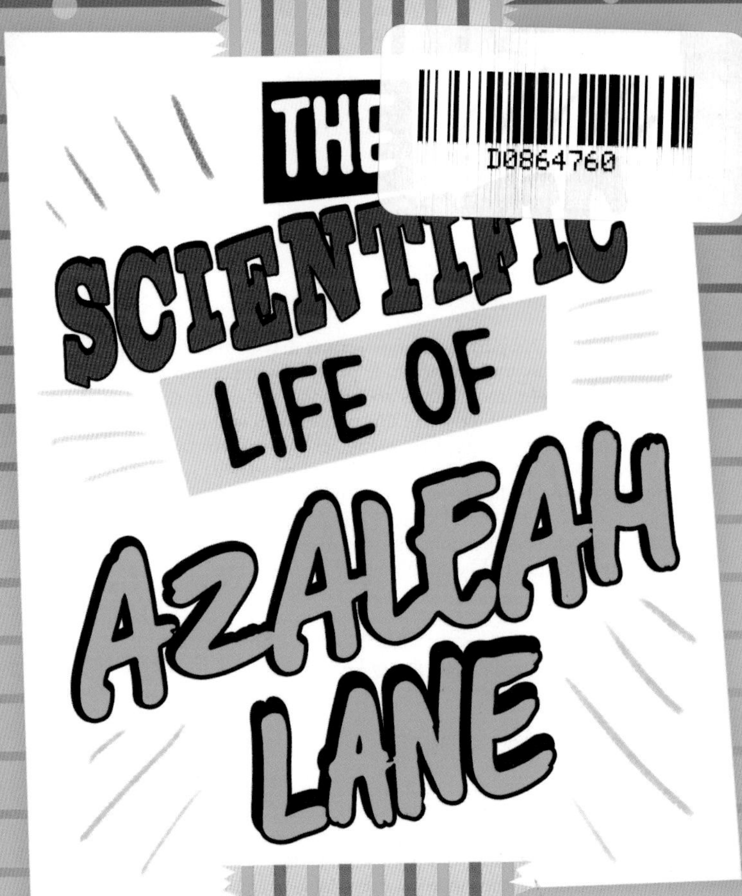

BY NIKKI SHANNON SMITH

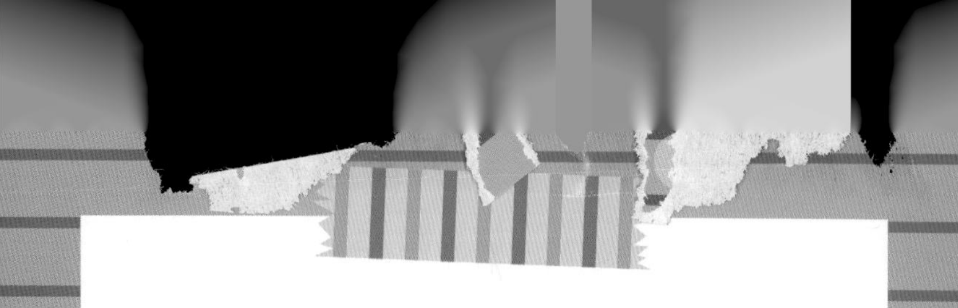

Raintree is an imprint of Capstone Global Library Limited, a company incorporated in England and Wales having its registered office at 264 Banbury Road, Oxford, OX2 7DY – Registered company number: 6695582

www.raintree.co.uk
myorders@raintree.co.uk

Designed by Kay Fraser
Original illustrations © Capstone Global Library Limited 2022
Originated by Capstone Global Library Ltd
Printed and bound in India

Image Credits: Shutterstock: Beskova Ekaterina, design element throughout.

ISBN 978 1 3982 3588 5

British Library Cataloguing in Publication Data
A full catalogue record for this book is available from the British Library.

CONTENTS

HEY, THERE! I'M AZALEAH!

I'm eight years old. My life is *amazing*. I live with my family: Mum, Dad, Nia and Tiana.

Mum has her very own restaurant here called Avec Amour. That means "with love" in French. She named it that because she adds love to everything she does.

My dad is a lawyer. He sues bad guys for a living. The bad guys work in big businesses that do things that hurt other people. But my dad makes them pay. He makes sure they're held responsible.

Tiana is my baby sister. She's four years old and pretty cute – most of the time. I like her a lot, even though she comes in my room too much. I also have an older sister called Nia. She's at secondary school and is always in her room. *Always.*

Mum's sister – my Auntie Sam – takes care of us when Mum and Dad are busy. I love Auntie Sam. She's never too tired to play and she likes to do art. She also likes adventures – my favourite!

Apart from my family, there are three main things you should know about me.

1. I'm curious . . . *not* nosy. (Despite what Nia says.)
2. I'm good at solving mysteries – very good.
3. I live in the White House!

OK . . . not the *real* White House. (The president of the United States lives there.) But my house is big and white, plus it has a great big living room and a nice garden. It's just as good as the real White House, if you ask me!

IT'S HARD TO BELIEVE THIS AMAZING LIFE ALL BELONGS TO ME, AZALEAH LANE!

CHAPTER 1

BAD MOOD MONDAY

I hopped out of bed on Monday morning like a kangaroo. I had been waiting all weekend for today!

Monday was special assembly day at school. And today's announcements were going to be *extra* special. Our headteacher, Ms Li, was picking a pupil from my class to be the STEM lab monitor for the week. Someone from a higher class had the first turn two weeks ago. Then Ms Li had picked someone from the the next class down. We had been waiting for a long time. But now it was going to be someone in my class's turn!

Please let Ms Li pick me, I thought.

I washed, got dressed, brushed my edges and ran to the kitchen. My parents were already there. Mum had her dressing gown on. She was staring out of the window with a cup of coffee in her hand. Dad was sitting at the table. He was wearing his dressing gown too. His eyes were droopy like he was about to fall asleep.

"Good morning!" I said.

I sat down with Dad. He smiled at me, but his lips were still asleep, so it was a very tiny smile.

Mum put homemade blueberry muffins, cantaloupe melon and orange juice on the table.

"Hi, Azaleah," she said.

"Guess what?" I asked.

Mum took a sip of coffee. Dad stared at his muffin. They didn't say anything.

As my parents didn't guess, I kept talking. "Today, Ms Li is picking someone in my class to be STEM lab monitor for the whole week. On Friday we all wrote our names on a ticket and put them in Ms Li's glitter box. Today, she's shaking the box, closing her eyes and picking out a name."

I crossed all of my fingers and hooked my thumbs together for good luck. I held them up and showed my hands to Dad.

He said, "Mmm hmmm."

I frowned. Something wasn't right. Dad and I were always the earliest early birds. But today he didn't have any energy at all.

"The STEM lab monitor is very important," I explained. "They take care of the STEM lab. They feed the animals and clean the cages and keep the lab clean. Sometimes they get to help Mr Aguilar, the STEM lab teacher, set up activities."

My parents still didn't answer me. Mum sat down and stared at her coffee. Dad ate his muffin. It reminded me of the time the batteries in my robot died. It got slower and slower, and then it stopped. My parents looked like they needed new batteries.

"What's wrong?" I asked.

"I'm just tired. I had a long night," said Mum. "I fed a hundred people last night."

I knew Mum had hosted a private party at her restaurant, Avec Amour. It was for the National Museum of African American History and Culture. But I didn't know it was that big. A hundred people was a lot!

"Wow, Mum," I said. "Avec Amour is getting famous!"

She nodded. Poor Mum was too tired to be excited. Owning the best restaurant around and being the best chef ever was hard work.

"You need a holiday, Mum," I said.

She smiled. "I'm on a mini-break now," she said. "I'm not working nights this week."

"Dad, are *you* okay?" I asked.

"I stayed up too late," he said. "I was reading a good book. Then your sister –"

Before Dad could finish, my little sister, Tiana, came into the kitchen. Her frown looked like one of those fish with a turned-down mouth. She was holding her favourite cuddly toy, Greenie, and her hair was sticking up all over her head. She tried to climb into Dad's lap, but he wouldn't let her.

"Sit in a chair and eat your breakfast, okay?" he said.

Tiana whined and sat in a chair. But instead of eating, she started crying.

"Why are you crying?" I asked.

Tiana looked at me and let out a long cry.

"She had a bad dream in the middle of the

night," said Dad. "I had to lie in her bed with her until she fell asleep again. It took a few hours. She's tired."

No wonder Dad looked like a zombie.

"Anyway," I said. I talked very loudly so they could hear me over Tiana's whining. "I hope I get to be the STEM lab monitor. There's a guinea pig named Harry, and he's so cute and fluffy. I would get to hold him and feed him!"

Tiana let out another big cry.

"Tiana, that's enough," said Mum.

I could tell Mum meant business. Tiana must have known it too because she closed her mouth and hugged Greenie.

Just then, our big sister, Nia, came in. Nia always looked great. She always had a cute outfit on. But not today. Today, Nia had on jeans and an old T-shirt that said *The World is My Stage*. She hadn't picked out her Afro, so it was flat on one side.

Nia was always trying different hairstyles. Lately she had been wearing it in an Afro because she was going to be Annie in her next school musical. Nia was always in a musical. Dad called her a triple threat. She could sing and act and dance. She would probably be famous one day. She was already

famous at her school.

"Guess what, Nia?" I said. "Today, Ms Li is choosing a new STEM lab monitor! It's going to be someone in my class. It could be *me*!"

Nia frowned and covered her ears. "Why is everyone being so loud? It's too early for this much noise."

My big sister was very dramatic. That's why she was such a good actor. But sometimes she was *too* dramatic, like right now. Right now she was dramatic *and* grumpy, and I knew why.

Nia had stayed up too late rehearsing for her musical. She had to memorise her lines and learn some songs. Last night, she had worked on her solo. It was a song about the sun coming out tomorrow. Her singing was so good, she actually sang me to sleep.

I sighed. My exciting Monday was feeling more like bad-mood Monday. Everyone in my house was complaining – except for me.

Hopefully school would be better than our kitchen. Hopefully Ms Li would announce my name, and I would be the best STEM lab monitor in the whole world.

I would impress Ms Li. Then, on Friday, when she announced weekly congratulations and recognitions, she would say my name again.

I could hear it now: "I would like to recognize Azaleah Lane for her fabulous work as the STEM lab monitor this week."

I couldn't wait to get to school. This might turn out to be the best day ever.

CHAPTER 2

SPECIAL ANNOUNCEMENTS

As soon as Dad dropped me off at school, I spotted my best friend, Rose, in the playground. She was already standing in line, even though the bell hadn't rung yet.

"Hi, Rose!" I shouted. "Today, Ms Li is picking someone for the STEM lab monitor job."

Rose grinned and did a little dance. "I know. It's finally our turn! I wonder who she'll pick."

The bell rang, and I jumped in line behind Rose. The rest of the class came running.

Somebody bumped someone else, and they started arguing. I could hear Terrance shouting about the STEM lab, even though he was all the way at the back of our line. Terrance was the most talkative person in my class.

Our teacher, Ms Johnson, came out and stood in front of us. She waited for everyone to calm down, but my class was too excited.

Ms Johnson let out a big sigh and started walking down the line. I knew she was giving reminders. That was when she had to tell you something she'd already told you before.

I peeked behind me and saw Ms Johnson stop and whisper something to Terrance. He nodded and stood very still.

I made sure I was nice and quiet because I didn't want to be late. Ms Li's announcements were first thing in the morning.

We finally got into our classroom. I sat at

my table and looked at the board. The first thing on the schedule was announcements. Rose sat down across from me. I grinned at her and pointed to the board. She smiled back.

Our class was very noisy. Lots of kids were talking about the STEM lab monitor. Before Ms Johnson could give out any more reminders, the intercom chime came on.

"Good morning, everyone," Ms Li said over the speaker. "Happy Monday. It's time for our special announcements."

The whispering in my classroom stopped. Everyone stared at the speaker in the front of our classroom.

Please let it be me, I thought.

"Today, I'll be drawing someone's name out of my special box," Ms Li continued. "That lucky person will be this week's STEM lab monitor!"

Rose and I looked at each other. Rose crossed her fingers. I crossed my fingers *and* thumbs.

"Can you hear that?" asked Ms Li.

The sound of paper rustling came through the speaker. "That's the sound of me shaking up the names in my box. I'm closing my eyes . . ."

My whole entire class held their breath.

" . . . and picking a name . . ."

There was silence while Ms Li picked a ticket.

"This week's STEM lab monitor is . . . Azaleah Lane in Ms Johnson's class!"

I grinned at Rose. She smiled with one side of her mouth. It looked like she was sad for herself and happy for me.

The other kids in my class sighed. I knew a lot of them wanted to be the STEM lab monitor. Some of them looked sad, so I worked very hard to be calm. I clapped a very soft clap and smiled at Ms Johnson. She smiled back.

"Azaleah, please go to the lab at break time. I'll pick another person next week," Ms Li finished. "Have a good day, everyone!"

Now I had to wait until morning break to check in with Mr Aguilar in the STEM lab. I couldn't wait to take Harry out of his cage and cuddle him. I would take good care of the lab. I was going to be an excellent monitor.

"I have a special announcement this

morning too," said Ms Johnson. "We are doing a special project this week. And it involves the STEM lab."

The whole class perked up. The sad kids looked less sad.

"What is it, Ms Johnson?" asked Terrance. He didn't even put his hand up.

"You'll be working in groups to make something called a chain-reaction machine," she said. "And –"

"What's a chain-reaction machine?" Terrance interrupted. He still didn't put his hand up.

Ms Johnson looked at him. I knew Terrance was about to get a reminder.

I was right. Ms Johnson said, "Please put your hand up, Terrance."

Terrance put his hand up. "What's a chain-reaction machine?" he asked.

"It uses energy and a chain reaction

to make something happen," explained Ms Johnson. "Have you ever set up dominoes in a line, and then pushed over the first one?"

The class nodded.

"What happens when you do that?" she asked.

Terrance put his hand up and shouted at the same time. "They all fall over!"

"That's right. The first domino knocks over the second one, and then the second one knocks over the third one. It continues like that until they've all fallen down," said Ms Johnson. "Each domino has energy. It can do work. When you knock one over, it gives its energy to the next domino. Then that one does work. Every time the energy makes something new happen, it's a chain reaction."

I never knew that energy was part of science. I always thought if you were moving around a lot it meant you had lots of energy. I put my hand up.

Ms Johnson called on me. "Yes, Azaleah?"

"Are we going to set up dominoes in a fancy pattern and knock them down?" I asked.

Ms Johnson shook her head. "Something even better," she said. "A chain-reaction machine is much cooler. We will use lots of different materials in the STEM lab to create a chain reaction. Your job will be to make a small bouncy ball land in a cup."

The class started to whisper about the project.

Rose leaned towards me. "I hope we're in the same group," she said.

I nodded and crossed my fingers and thumbs at Rose. "Me too," I said.

"Let's watch a chain-reaction machine at work," said Ms Johnson. She turned off the lights and started a video.

Music played while a girl in the video pulled a string to start a chain reaction. I could see the energy going from one thing to another. Blocks fell over, gears spun and a roll of toilet paper bumped a tennis ball. The ball rolled down a path and plopped straight into a rubbish bin. The class clapped.

"This is going to be fun!" yelled Terrance.

Ms Johnson turned on the lights. "Now let's

talk about your group assignments. I've split you up into six groups of four."

She started reading our names from a piece of paper. I waited to hear my name. Finally, she said, "Group four will be Azaleah, Rose . . ."

Rose and I grinned at each other. This was definitely turning into the best day ever!

". . . Jamal and Terrance," finished Ms Johnson.

My grin disappeared. I hoped Terrance wouldn't get our group in trouble with his talking.

Ms Johnson finished reading the group assignments. "Now," she said, "let's break into our groups. You have thirty minutes."

"I thought we were going to the STEM lab," yelled Terrance.

Everyone looked at Terrance, including Ms Johnson. She looked like she was taking three calming breaths. She had taught us to do that when we were getting upset.

"We will go tomorrow," Ms Johnson said slowly. "We usually only go on Fridays, so I had to sign up for extra time."

Rose and I made our way to table four. I looked at the clock. Thirty minutes with talkative Terrance . . . and thirty minutes until I started my job as STEM lab monitor!

CHAPTER 3

SERIOUS BUSINESS

Our group sat down at table four. Rose and I sat next to each other, and Jamal sat next to Terrance.

Jamal smiled at me. I was glad he was in our group. He was very clever and worked very hard. One time Ms Johnson let us make animal habitat dioramas. Jamal's was one of the best. He was the only one in the class who made a naked mole rat.

"This is going to be so much fun," said Terrance. "I already know what our machine is going to look like."

Ms Johnson rang the bell that meant silence, so I couldn't answer Terrance. But I wanted to. I wanted to tell him that he didn't know what our machine was going to look like because we hadn't talked about it yet. Ms Johnson always said groups had to *discuss* ideas first.

"Here are the directions for our group planning time," Ms Johnson said.

"We don't need time to plan," Terrance whispered to us. "We're ready to build now."

Rose and Jamal frowned. I took three calming breaths.

Ms Johnson put chart paper up on the board. It had a list of all of the supplies in the craft area. There were blocks, toilet paper rolls and all kinds of other things. Then she added another piece of paper to the board.

"From now until breaktime, I want you to do these three things," she said.

I read the chart. It said:

Group Discussion

1. *Discuss your building ideas. Take turns in speaking.*
2. *Talk about which materials you might like to use.*
3. *Work together to draw an idea of what your machine might look like.*

"Jamal, you can go first," I said. "What's your idea?"

Jamal opened his mouth, but before he could talk, Terrance did. "We are using the blocks, the racetracks, some tape, a cup and a ball," he said.

Rose said, "I was thinking –"

Terrance interrupted. He was worse than Tiana – and she was a *major* interrupter.

"What we do," he said, "is stack the blocks and lay the tracks over them. Then the ball can roll down the track and land in the cup."

Rose's cheeks went pink. Her cheeks did that when she laughed really hard. They also did that when she was really angry.

"We're supposed to *discuss* the idea," I said.

Rose and Jamal nodded.

Terrance said, "We don't need to. My idea is really good."

"We should use more materials," said Jamal. "Then we can make the machine do different things, like in the video."

"We don't need to," said Terrance again.

Terrance reminded me of a parrot that could only say one thing.

"Read step one," I said. "Take turns in speaking. That means we have to listen to *everyone's* ideas."

Jamal and Terrance looked at something behind me. I turned round in my seat, and my eyes went big. The headteacher, Ms Li, was standing right behind me.

"Good morning," Ms Li said. "I thought I would visit Ms Johnson's classroom this morning. I heard you were starting an exciting project."

My face felt hot. I wondered if my cheeks had turned pink like Rose's. Ms Li had probably heard us arguing.

Ms Li smiled at me. "Congratulations on being the STEM lab monitor, Azaleah," she said.

I smiled back. "Thank you."

Ms Li walked round and talked to each group. Then the morning break bell rang, and Ms Li left. All of the other groups handed their drawings to Ms Johnson.

My group didn't have a drawing. My group hadn't even finished step one.

I was happy about one thing, though. It was breaktime. And that meant it was time for me to report for duty!

I jumped up from the table and said goodbye to Rose. Then I fast-walked to the STEM lab. When I got there, I peeked through the door.

"Hi, Azaleah!" said Mr Aguilar. "Come on in!"

Mr Aguilar was one of the nicest teachers at my school. He was also very interesting. Sometimes he showed us science experiments where he mixed different liquids. They bubbled and smoked. They were called chemical reactions.

Mr Aguilar pointed to a list on the wall. "This is the lab-monitor checklist," he said. "The top part is for morning break. The bottom is for afternoon break. Being the monitor is serious business. You're not just keeping the room tidy and helping me set things up. You're responsible for the animals."

I nodded and started following all of the steps.

1. *Give Snappy the turtle a lettuce leaf and three carrot slices from the fridge.*
2. *Feed the fish a tiny pinch of food.*
3. *Put one scoop of guinea pig food in Harry's dish.*
4. *Fasten the cage door!*
5. *If you have extra time, help keep the STEM lab clean.*

I saved the best – Harry the guinea pig – for last.

"Can I take Harry out of his cage?" I asked.

"Just for a minute," said Mr Aguilar. "Make sure you close the latch and tie the string back on the door when you've finished."

"Why is there a string?" I asked.

Mr Aguilar chuckled. "Harry is a bit of an escape artist. He's worked out the latch."

"Oh no," I said. "I'll be extra careful."

I picked up Harry and rubbed his fur on my face. He was the cutest little guinea pig I'd ever seen.

I gave him a very gentle guinea pig hug and kissed his head. Then I tucked him back in his cage and fastened the latch.
I remembered to tie the string around the door.

When I looked up, Mr Aguilar was watching me. "You did a really good job,

Azaleah. Thank you for being so careful with Harry."

I smiled. Being the STEM room monitor was just as amazing as I thought it would be. I couldn't wait to hold Harry again at afternoon break. I was going to be the best monitor Mr Aguilar had ever seen!

* * *

I thought about Harry during writing time. I thought about Harry at lunchtime. I thought about Harry's cute face while Ms Johnson read us a story. At art time, I even drew Harry.

Finally, it was afternoon break. I ran to the STEM room. I went to say hi to Harry straight away. I put my face up to his cage, but there was a great big problem waiting for me. . . .

Harry was gone!

CHAPTER 4

HELP!

"Mr Aguilar!" I yelled.

I searched all around the lab. I couldn't see Harry anywhere.

Mr Aguilar came hurrying out of the lab storage cupboard. "What's wrong, Azaleah?" he asked.

I pointed to Harry's empty cage. "Harry is gone!"

"I don't believe it," Mr Aguilar said. "He worked out the string? It must have happened while I was out of the classroom."

I felt tears burning my eyes. *Maybe I didn't*

tie the string tight enough, I thought. *What if something bad happened to Harry?*

"Where could he be?" I asked.

"Let's not panic. He can't be far," said Mr Aguilar. "Have a look round the room. This isn't the first time Harry has escaped. I don't know how he gets down from the workbench, but we always find him."

I tried to stay calm. I moved the papers and baskets and boxes that were on the workbench with Harry's cage. He wasn't there.

I looked behind the blinds on the window at the end of the workbench. No Harry.

I walked around the STEM lab. I looked under the shelves. I looked in the corners. I looked by the rubbish bin. I even looked under Mr Aguilar's desk. But I couldn't find Harry.

The bell rang. That meant break was over. I hadn't done anything on the afternoon list. I hadn't changed Snappy's water or put hay in

Harry's cage. I hadn't put the craft bins away for the day either.

"Mr Aguilar, what should I do?" I asked.

"Let's Harry-proof the room before you go," he said.

"Harry-proof?" I repeated.

Mr Aguilar nodded. "There are things we can do to keep him safe. First, let's unplug the

radio and the pencil sharpener so Harry won't chew the cords."

"Should we pick up pencils and paper scraps so Harry won't eat them?" I asked.

"Good idea, Azaleah," said Mr Aguilar.

He helped me clean the floor. When it was time for me to leave, Mr Aguilar locked the door.

"This way, no one can come in. And if the door is shut, Harry can't leave," explained Mr Aguilar. "I'm sure he'll go back to his cage when he gets hungry. That's what he did last time."

I hoped Mr Aguilar was right.

When I got back to my classroom, Rose stared at me. "Azaleah, what's wrong?" she asked. "You look scared."

I didn't want Rose to know Harry was missing. I didn't want anyone to know. They would think I was a bad STEM lab monitor.

"Nothing," I said.

During maths, I did my times tables with my head on my desk. But I was so busy worrying about Harry I couldn't finish them. When it was time to go home, Ms Johnson told me to do the rest for homework.

Mum and Tiana picked me up from school. Tiana talked about her best friend, Kevin. When we picked up Nia, she talked about her rehearsal. Mum told us about a new recipe she was trying.

I stayed quiet in the car all the way home. Nobody remembered about the STEM lab monitor announcement. I was glad because I didn't want to talk about it.

* * *

At dinner that night, I was still worrying about Harry. I must have been frowning, because Tiana stared at me.

"Azaleah, are you sad?" she asked.

Mum turned from the cooker and looked at me. Dad and Nia looked at me too.

I burst into tears. "This was the worst day ever."

"What happened?" asked Dad.

"Oh, the STEM lab!" said Nia. "Are you sad because you didn't get picked today?"

"I *did* get picked," I cried. "But Harry escaped. HE'S MISSING! And it's all my fault!"

"The guinea pig?" asked Mum.

I nodded. "And that's not all. We started a group project. We were supposed to plan for the STEM lab tomorrow. But Terrance bossed us around and wouldn't let anybody talk," I said.

Mum handed me a napkin to wipe my face. I told my family all about my whole horrible day.

"What are you going to do?" asked Dad.

I thought for a minute. "I'm going to find Harry," I said. "But I don't know what to do about Terrance."

"Use your words," said Tiana. "Say *NO, Terrance.* Yell *no* lots of times."

"I don't think he'll listen," I said. Plus, I knew that would start an argument.

"Pretend you're a character who solves problems," said Nia.

"I'm a real person who solves problems," I said. "But I don't know how to solve this one."

"Talk to Ms Johnson about Terrance," said Mum.

"Talk to *Terrance* about Terrance," said Dad. "Do it privately."

I didn't think any of those things would work. Reminders from Ms Johnson didn't even work with Terrance.

"Can I be excused?" I asked.

My parents looked at each other. Mum nodded at me.

I spent the rest of the night alone in my bedroom. I finished my maths and put on my pyjamas. Then I got a book and climbed into bed. I read until Mum came to tuck me in.

She gave me a kiss and pulled my covers up to my chin. "Sleep tight," she said. "Tomorrow will be better."

I did not sleep tight. I thought about my group project. I thought about Terrance. I didn't want to tell on him. He might be angry.

I decided to use my words – but not privately. Maybe we could have a group talk. I could help Terrance listen to all of us.

But mostly I thought about poor, lost Harry. I hoped he wasn't cold. I hoped Mr Aguilar was right and Harry would go back to his cage when he got hungry. Maybe he already had. Maybe Harry was fast asleep in his cage.

I wrapped myself in my blanket and closed my eyes. Down the corridor I could hear Nia singing about the sun coming out tomorrow.

I hope she's right, I thought. Then I fell asleep.

CHAPTER 5

WORDS

When I got to school, I went straight to the STEM lab. I wanted to see if Harry was back. The door was locked. I knocked, but no one answered.

I stood there and waited. When the bell rang Mr Aguilar still wasn't there. I had to go and line up.

Rose was already standing in line. "There you are!" she said. "You're late today."

I smiled at Rose but didn't say anything. Looking at my best friend made me think about the group project. And that made me think about Terrance. I could hear his voice all the way from the back of the line.

Ms Johnson walked us into the classroom. She waited for us to go quiet. "Today is our first day in the STEM lab," she said.

Some of the kids clapped. Terrance said, "Yesssss!"

"You will have three days to build your machines. On Friday, you will share your work with the class." Ms Johnson pointed to the charts on the board. "Don't forget, this is group work. Take turns. Share your ideas."

We lined up and went to the STEM lab. The door was unlocked, but Mr Aguilar wasn't in there. He had put up a little screen in front of the animals, though. He did that sometimes if the lab was going to be busy. He didn't want Harry and Snappy to get scared. The problem was, I couldn't see if Harry was there or not.

I sighed and sat at a table with my group. Crates were set up all around the room. There were building blocks and racetracks and toilet paper rolls. There were dominoes, tape, cups, balls and all kinds of other things too. There were even boards leaning against the workbench for us.

Wow! I thought. *Mr Aguilar has thought of everything!*

"Look at all this!" said Jamal. "We can make something really complicated."

Terrance shook his head. "It doesn't need to be complicated."

Rose said, "Let's pick our materials."

"Yeah!" said Jamal. "We didn't get to finish that part yesterday."

"I've finished that part already," said Terrance. "Rose and Azaleah, you can get the tape, a cup and a ball. Jamal and I can get the blocks and racetracks."

I could see why Tiana had told me to say, "No, Terrance." *No* was exactly what I felt like saying.

Rose, Jamal and I looked at each other. We didn't say anything. We also didn't go and get the materials. This was the perfect time to use my words.

"I think we should talk about it first," I said. Jamal and Rose nodded.

"We don't need to," Terrance said. "We already have a plan."

Terrance was making me angry. I took three calming breaths.

"We are supposed to share ideas," I said.

Terrance ignored me. He stood up, walked to the crates and got some blocks. Then he came back and sat down.

I looked at the other groups. They were all carrying things to their tables. Some of them were smiling. One group had already started building.

Rose stomped over to the bins. She got tape, a cup and a ball. When she came back her cheeks were very pink.

Jamal stayed where he was. He didn't go and get anything.

I could tell Jamal was not going to listen to Terrance. He also was not going to use his words.

"Jamal," said Terrance, "you forgot the racetracks."

Jamal didn't answer, so I did. "We want to tell you our ideas," I said.

"Let's just start," said Terrance. He started stacking the blocks.

I needed a break from Terrance. I headed over to the workbench to peek behind the screen. I wanted to see if Harry was back.

"Azaleah!" said Terrance very loudly. "We're supposed to be working together."

I turned around. Ms Johnson was looking at me. I frowned and went back to my group.

All around us, the other groups had started their machines. They had all kinds of materials. They were taking turns adding things to the machines. They were talking and smiling. One machine fell over. The group laughed.

Everyone is having fun but us, I thought.

Rose rolled the ball on the floor between her hands. Jamal had got a piece of paper. I peeked at what he was drawing. It looked like his own plan for a machine.

Jamal's plan had really good chain reactions. It showed dominoes falling and hitting a toilet paper roll. The roll bumped over a pile of straws. He wasn't finished yet, but I liked his idea.

"That's awesome, Jamal!" I said. "Rose,

look at this."

"Oh!" she said. "That's really good."

Terrance didn't even look. He kept stacking blocks and putting racetracks on top. He was talking to himself.

"First, the tracks will be on the tall blocks," he said. "Then, the stacks will get short. The tracks will go downhill. We can put the ball at the top. It will roll down and land in the cup."

"Terrance," I said, "where is the chain reaction? One thing is supposed to make another thing happen."

Rose and Jamal nodded.

"The hill is going to make the ball roll. Weren't you listening to me?" he asked.

Ms Johnson clapped her hands. That meant it was time to stop.

Everyone lined up for morning break except me. I needed to stay and do my STEM lab monitor job. I was glad my class was leaving. I could finally check Harry's cage.

As soon as everyone else was gone, I had a look behind the screen. Harry was still missing.

"Oh, no," I said.

I hurried over and closed the door to the lab to keep Harry inside. I fed the fish and Snappy. Then I got on my hands and knees.
I crawled around on the floor.

"Harry, where are you?" I whispered. "Please come back."

I wished Mr Aguilar would come back too. I needed help.

I didn't see any sign of Harry, but I did have an idea. If Harry was still in the lab, I should leave his food on the floor for him.

I left five pellets near Mr Aguilar's desk. And while I was there, I found a clue – guinea pig droppings!

Usually poo on the floor would be bad news. But not this time. This time, poo was good news. It meant Harry was still in here somewhere!

CHAPTER 6

HARRY SITUATION

For the rest of the day I focused on my work. I finished my writing and had time to illustrate my story. I played with Rose at lunchtime.

Finally, it was afternoon break. When I got to the lab, Mr Aguilar was sitting at his desk and staring at his computer.

"Hi, Azaleah," he said.

"Is Harry back?" I asked.

Mr Aguilar's face looked a tiny bit sad and a lot stressed. "Not yet."

"Mr Aguilar, are you okay?" I asked.

He gave me the same smile Mum did when she was extra tired. "Yes," he said. "I've just been busy getting kids ready for the Science Investigation Station. I'm a bit tired."

My big sister, Nia, had done the Investigation Station. It was a huge contest. The kids got to be science detectives. They did science investigations and solved problems. The school that won even got a trophy.

I nodded at him. "Did you see the droppings?" I asked.

Mr Aguilar shook his head. "No! Where?"

"Right by your shoe," I said.

Mr Aguilar looked down and nodded. He seemed happy about the poo too. "You have good eyes."

I started to clean Harry's cage. It was one of my afternoon jobs. I had to pull out the tray at the bottom and dump out the shavings. Then I had to put in new ones. I also changed

Harry's water. Just then I noticed something interesting.

The string on Harry's cage was not untied. It was *chewed*. This was not my fault after all! I had been so upset yesterday I hadn't even noticed. Harry really was an escape artist!

"Look, Mr Aguilar." I pointed at the string.

"That little rascal," said Mr Aguilar.

"He outsmarted me again!"

I decided to do some investigating. Maybe there were other things I hadn't noticed yesterday.

I walked around the classroom. I had to step over a machine. I noticed one of the boards from yesterday hadn't been used. It was still leaning against the workbench like a ramp.

"Maybe Harry climbed down one of the boards," I said.

Mr Aguilar rubbed his beard. "I bet you're right."

I crouched on the floor next to the end of the board. I pretended I was a guinea pig.

Where would I go? I wondered.

Since Harry's droppings were near the desk, I crawled that way. Then I found another clue!

"Mr Aguilar, two of the food pellets I left

are gone!" I exclaimed.

"You're quite the detective, Azaleah," he said. "Keep going with your investigation."

I crawled all over the room. I had to crawl around our machines very carefully. I didn't want to knock them over. Some of them were already tall. One of them had a block dangling from a string. Another one used a kitchen towel roll as a chute for the ball.

I didn't stop crawling until I got to the bookshelf on the other side of the room. It was a lot of work.

I bet Harry is really tired, I thought.

On the bottom shelf I spotted an interesting book. It was called *Raising Your Guinea Pig*. That gave me another idea.

"Mr Aguilar, can I borrow your guinea pig book?" I asked.

I knew that scientists did lots of reading

to learn new things. They called it research. Maybe I could learn something that would help me find Harry.

"Of course," he said. "The bell rang, though. You need to hurry to class."

I hadn't even heard the bell. I had been very focused on looking for clues. I took the book and stood up.

Before I left, I looked at the machines around the room. The other groups were doing really well.

Then I stared at ours. It was not creative. It was not complicated. There were no chain reactions. It wasn't even tall. It would not impress anyone.

I sighed. I was not close to solving the Terrance problem. Not at all. But I might be closer to solving the guinea pig mystery. And that was a good start.

CHAPTER 7

RESEARCH

That night after dinner, I ran to my room. I pulled the guinea pig book out of my backpack. I wanted to find as many clues as I could.

The first chapter was all about what guinea pigs looked like. I already knew what Harry looked like, but I read it anyway. I learned that some guinea pigs don't have fur!

The next chapter was about how to look after a guinea pig. It was very interesting. Harry ate pellets and hay. The book said guinea pigs also liked fruits and vegetables.

I wonder if Mr Aguilar gives Harry treats, I thought.

That gave me a good idea. If I put out treats, maybe Harry would come and get them. Then I could catch him and put him in his cage.

I grabbed a piece of paper. I started a list of guinea pig treats. I wrote:

- greens
- apples
- sweet peppers
- pears
- broccoli

I also read a very interesting fact. Guinea pigs are nocturnal. They are supposed to be awake at night. But Harry was always awake during the day.

Maybe that's because he lives in a classroom with so many visitors, I thought.

I added *nocturnal* to my paper. Then I ran back downstairs. Mum was in the kitchen chopping salt pork.

"What are you doing, Mum?" I asked.

She smiled at me. "I'm just chopping some pork and some cabbage for tomorrow."

I couldn't believe my luck! "Mum, did you know guinea pigs like cabbage?"

"No, I didn't," said Mum.

"Can I have a leaf for Harry?" I asked.

Mum handed me two big cabbage leaves from a gigantic pile. I thought about my list. Greens were yummy, but apples were sweet. Harry might like apples for dessert.

I waited until Mum finished cutting the meat, so she wouldn't cut herself. Then I asked, "Mum, can you please cut me a piece of apple?"

"It's a little late for a snack, Azaleah," said Mum.

I giggled. “Not for me. For Harry!”

Mum laughed too. She cut two slices of apple for Harry. I put the cabbage and apples in a plastic bag. I saved them in the fridge for tomorrow. Then I kissed Mum and ran back to my room.

I climbed into bed with my guinea pig book. Chapter three was about guinea pig behaviour. It said guinea pigs are social beings. They like to be around people. They like to play. They liked to have a nap time and a mealtime.

Maybe that's why I have to feed Harry at morning break, I thought. *It's his mealtime.*

The book also said guinea pigs like to hide. Harry was certainly very good at that!

I had lots of good information. I also had guinea pig treats. Tomorrow, I would do some more detective work. I couldn't wait!

CHAPTER 8

CLOSED

When I got to school the next morning, I had a plan. I went straight to the STEM lab again. Mr Aguilar was already there, taking microscopes out of a box.

"Is Harry back?" I asked.

Mr Aguilar shook his head. "I'm starting to worry. He's never been gone this long."

I pulled out the plastic bag and held it up so Mr Aguilar could see. "I brought treats!"

"Hmm . . . ," said Mr Aguilar. "That's a good idea."

"Can I put them on the floor?" I asked. "Maybe Harry will come out and get them."

"Yes," said Mr Aguilar. "I have to get my work done, so I won't be able to help this morning."

I put one chunk of cabbage near the desk where Harry had left droppings. Mr Aguilar had cleaned them up. I put an apple slice near the board leaning against the workbench.

The bell rang. I had to go to class. I decided to save the rest of the treats for later.

Straight away, I noticed Ms Johnson had put up a new poster. It said *Leaders From Around the World*. It had pictures of lots of world leaders on it.

Terrance noticed it too. "Wow!" he yelled. "Where did you get that?"

Ms Johnson said, "Don't forget to put your hand up, Terrance. Ms Li got one of these posters for every classroom."

Terrance raised his hand. Then he talked, even though Ms Johnson hadn't asked him to. "I got to vote with my parents," he said.

I raised my hand. But I waited until Ms Johnson called on me. When she did, I asked, "Can kids vote?"

Ms Johnson shook her head. "Not in government elections. Only adults can vote for president. They can also vote for other leaders, like mayors. Voting makes things more fair. Every vote counts."

"I didn't really vote," said Terrance. "I only watched my parents. But the people there gave me a sticker. It said *I voted*."

"Please wait to be asked to speak, Terrance," said Ms Johnson. Then she said, "Azaleah, there are other ways kids can vote."

"How?" I asked.

"Let's vote right now," said Ms Johnson. "Our turn in the STEM lab is after break today. We are about to go out for PE. Let's vote on what to play: football or basketball."

The class cheered.

"Put your hand up if you want to play basketball," said Ms Johnson.

A few people put their hands up.

Next she said, "Put your hand up if you want to play football."

Most people, including me, put their hands up the second time. Football won.

I liked voting. It was fair.

But behind me, I heard someone say, "But I wanted to play basketball."

"Sometimes you don't win," Ms Johnson said. "But at least your vote counted."

That gave me the most fantastic idea in the world. My group could vote about our project! We could vote to take turns sharing ideas *or* to use Terrance's idea. Plus, Terrance wouldn't even have to listen to us. He could see our hands!

* * *

I was so excited I skipped all the way to the STEM lab at morning break. Mr Aguilar was looking through a box on the workbench. The outside said *Imagination Station*. I stood next to him and peeked into Harry's cage.

"Still no Harry?" I asked.

Mr Aguilar let out the kind of sigh Mum did when she was extra tired. "Still no Harry," he said.

Even though there was no Harry, I had to do my other jobs. I fed Snappy and the fish. Then I decided to check the floor for more clues. First, I looked at the apple slice. It was exactly where I left it. Then, I looked at the cabbage.

"Mr Aguilar!" I shouted. "Something has been nibbling at the cabbage! It's even moved a little bit!"

He squatted down next to me. "That's great!" he said. "While your class is in here, keep an eye out for Harry. Hopefully, he'll come back for the rest of it."

After the bell, my class walked into the STEM lab. Everyone sat next to their machines and got straight to work.

Terrance said, "Okay, let's get the rest of the racetracks done."

I said, "I think we should take a group vote. Just like we did in class."

Rose's eyes got very big, and she nodded. Jamal grinned.

Terrance said, "We don't need –"

But before Terrance could finish, I said, "We have two choices. We can use Terrance's idea, or we can take turns and come up with a new idea."

Terrance frowned at us.

"Put your hand up for Terrance's idea," I said.

Terrance raised his hand. His frown got even bigger when we didn't put ours up.

"Put your hand up for a new group idea," I said.

I raised my hand. So did Rose and Jamal.

"But –" said Terrance.

"We voted," said Jamal.

"A new group idea won," I said.

"Sometimes you don't win," said Rose. "But at least your vote counted."

Terrance crossed his arms.

"But guess what, Terrance?" I said. "You are part of our group. You get to share ideas too."

Terrance didn't look happy, but he didn't argue. Our group took turns in sharing ideas. Jamal showed us the drawing he had been working on. Rose said she wanted the ball to go through a toilet paper roll tunnel.

I said, "That's a really good idea. And I like the way Jamal's plan uses dominoes to make the ball start rolling."

Terrance said, "We can put my part at the end of Jamal's idea. The ball can go through Rose's tunnel. And then it can go down my hill."

"Oooo, and then we can make the ball

fly off the cliff and into the cup!" I said.

Everyone in my group clapped. We all smiled. Even Terrance! We went to the crates together to get our materials.

On the way back to our table, I looked around. I didn't see Harry, but I did see that some of the groups had almost finished their machines.

"We'd better hurry," I said. "We have to catch up and finish by tomorrow."

With everyone working together instead of arguing, we were doing a good job. Then Mr Aguilar called me to his desk.

"Azaleah," he whispered, "have you had any luck spotting Harry?"

I shook my head. "What about you?"

"No," he admitted. "But I just got an email from Ms Li. I mentioned this morning that Harry was missing. She wants us to close the lab until we find him."

Close the lab? I thought. *That's bad news.*

My class wouldn't be able to finish our projects. And everyone would find out that Harry was missing. Even worse, they would all know it happened while I was the monitor.

"But why do we have to close the whole lab?" I asked.

"Well, Ms Li has to think about our health and safety," Mr Aguilar explained. "If Harry is scared, he might bite someone."

I looked at the floor. I wished I could have just one more day in the lab. We could probably finish our project. And maybe I could find Harry too.

"I need to tell the class," said Mr Aguilar. He walked to the front of the room. "May I have your attention, please?"

The class stopped talking and looked up. Mr Aguilar didn't often make announcements. Everyone waited to see what he would say.

“I have some bad news,” he said. “Harry is missing.”

The whole class turned and looked at me. Their eyes were big. My face got very, very hot. I hid it in my hands.

Somebody asked, “Did Azaleah lose him?” I didn’t know who it was, because I couldn’t see.

“No, it’s not Azaleah’s fault,” Mr Aguilar said. “Harry chewed through the string and let himself out. He did it when no one was looking."

All the kids started talking at the same time. Ms Johnson clapped her hands and said, "Quiet, please."

Mr Aguilar continued. "I have to close the lab until we find Harry. We need to keep him safe. And we need to keep you safe."

"Please stand up carefully," Ms Johnson said. "Walk slowly to the door."

The class sadly lined up at the door. I could hear them whispering. Somebody asked, "What about our projects?"

Ms Johnson didn't answer.

"Azaleah, please stay for a minute," said Mr Aguilar.

Ms Johnson led everyone out of the STEM lab. I stayed behind.

"Since the lab is closed, there's no afternoon shift today," said Mr Aguilar.

"I'll take care of your jobs. Why don't you come back in the morning?"

I nodded. I couldn't believe the STEM lab was closed. I couldn't do my afternoon jobs. And my group couldn't finish our project, even though we had a good idea.

So much for congratulations and recognitions, I thought.

CHAPTER 9

SPECIAL PERMISSION

At dinnertime, I told my family what had happened in the STEM lab. First, I told them about voting. Then, I told them Harry was still missing.

"I'm proud of you, Azaleah," said Mum. "Voting was a good solution."

"What about Harry?" asked Tiana. "What if you never, ever find him?"

"She will," said Dad. "Azaleah is a detective."

Dad was right. I was a detective. And I never gave up. I *would* find Harry. But I'd have to get back into the STEM lab first.

I finished my dinner and asked, "Mum, can I use some things from the fridge?"

Mum nodded, so I put together a dish of fresh food for Harry. Luckily, Mum kept our fridge full of everything. We had all of the things on my list of favourite guinea pig foods.

I also had a new idea. *Maybe I need to change the way I put out the food*?

"Dad, can you take me to school early tomorrow?" I asked.

"Why?" he asked.

"I want to do some detective work in the STEM lab," I explained.

"Will the teacher be there?" he asked.

I thought about that for a minute. "I think so. Mr Aguilar has a lot to do. He's getting ready for the Investigation Station."

"Alright," said Dad. "Nia has rehearsal before school anyway. I can drop you off on the way."

I gave him a great big hug. Now I just had to wait until the morning.

* * *

When I got to school, the corridors were still quiet. I could hear music coming from the STEM lab. That was good news.

I opened the door. Mr Brannan was in there. He was the school caretaker.

"Azaleah, you're very early," he said.

"I know. I have some work to do. Is Mr Aguilar here?" I asked.

Mr Brannan shook his head and emptied the small rubbish can into his big rubbish bag.

"Would it be okay if I come in?" I asked.

Mr Brannan wore glasses that made his eyes look extra big. He looked at me for a long time. Then he said, "I admire hard workers. Come on in."

I went in and checked Harry's cage. He still wasn't there, so I got straight to work. First, I crawled around on the floor. I looked for more droppings. There were some by the desk. And the cabbage was gone.

Harry was busy last night, I thought.

I took out my dish of treats. If there were fresh treats scattered all over the place, Harry would smell them. He would eat the ones that were closest. Then I could tell where he was.

Just then, Mr Aguilar came in. He looked at Mr Brannan, then at me. "Good morning, Azaleah," he said.

"I gave her special permission to come in," Mr Brannan explained.

"Hi, Mr Aguilar. I have a plan," I said.

I told him what I was doing. He nodded.

"It might work," he said. "I'll let you finish, but then you need to go. You aren't really supposed to be in here."

By the time school started, I had little piles of treats in all four corners of the room. I also put treats in the middle of the room. There were a few piles in between our machines too.

"See you at break, Mr Aguilar," I said.

"Okay," he said. "But only to check in. The lab is still closed, remember."

I went to class, but I couldn't concentrate. The whole time Ms Johnson taught maths, I thought about Harry. I felt bad I hadn't found him yet.

I knew I had the right treats for him. And the guinea pig book said guinea pigs like to be social. I couldn't work out why Harry wasn't coming out to see me. There had to be something I wasn't thinking of.

Finally, morning break came. This time, I didn't hurry to the STEM lab. I was a little bit nervous.

What if my idea didn't work? What if Harry never comes out? I worried.

When I got there, Mr Aguilar was waiting. "Azaleah, I really need your help. Ms Li said it was okay. I have to get ready for a lesson. Will you please feed Snappy and the fish?" he asked.

I did what Mr Aguilar asked me to do. Then I started checking my piles of food. The ones in the corners looked the same. The pile in the middle looked the same too. I started checking the piles near the machines.

I had put three piles of food near the projects. The first one looked the same as it did this morning. But the second one had almost gone!

Harry was busy last night and *this morning,* I thought.

"Oh my goodness!" I said. "Why didn't I think of that before?"

"Think of what?" asked Mr Aguilar.

"Guinea pigs are nocturnal! When I was crawling all over the STEM lab, I got tired," I said. "A tiny guinea pig would get *very* tired. Especially if he was awake all night and came out to eat during the day. I don't think Harry's hiding from us. I think he's sleeping!"

Mr Aguilar rubbed his beard. He leaned forwards and watched me.

I looked at the machine near the pile Harry had munched on. It was supposed to look like a castle. There was a round tower made out of blocks and a little door at the bottom.

A door just big enough for a guinea pig to crawl through, I realized.

"What if Harry is sound asleep in a machine?" I shouted.

I laid on the floor and pressed my face down. I looked through the machine's little door. Inside, there was Harry, curled into

a little ball. He was fast asleep.

"Harry!" I said. "There you are!"

Harry woke up and twitched his nose at me. He crawled out. I picked him up and snuggled him. I kissed his head.

"Have you been finding new cosy spots to sleep in every day?" I asked him.

"Wow, Azaleah," said Mr Aguilar. "I didn't even see that opening. I would never have looked under there!"

"That's okay," I said. "I'm a detective. I investigate. I solve mysteries all the time."

Mr Aguilar laughed. "You're a *scientist*! I can't wait to have you on my Investigation Station team when you're older!"

I put Harry back in his nice clean cage. I shut the latch on the door. I was about to tie the string around the door, but Mr Aguilar handed me something.

"Use this wire," he said. "I don't think

Harry can chew through this!"

We laughed. Harry curled back into a ball and went to sleep. He looked like he was glad to be home.

When the bell rang, Mr Aguilar said, "Let me call Ms Johnson. I need your help. Then maybe your class can come in."

Ms Johnson told Mr Aguilar it was okay for me to stay. He told her we found Harry. I could hear my class clapping and cheering all the way through the phone!

Before he hung up, he said, "You can bring the class to the lab in ten minutes. Azaleah and I need to make sure the floor is clean."

Mr Aguilar and I checked the whole lab for droppings. We cleaned up after Harry, and Mr Aguilar used special wipes on the floor. As soon as we finished, my class came in.

"Well done finding Harry!" said Rose.

"Yeah," said Jamal. "Thanks to you, we get

to finish our project."

"I heard you had to pick up Harry's poo," said Terrance. He scrunched up his face and laughed.

"I did. But at least he's back home!" I said.

My group laughed. And then we got to work.

Ms Johnson said we could stay there until lunchtime. Some of the groups finished early, and she took them outside to play. Mr Aguilar stayed in the lab with the groups that were still working.

My group was the last one in the lab. We were still trying to get the last part of our machine to work.

"You only have five minutes left," said Mr Aguilar.

"I'll hold the ball still," said Terrance. "Jamal, you and Azaleah get the track just right. Rose, you get the cup and put it exactly where the ball bounces."

We all took our places. Terrance let go of the ball. It rolled through the tunnel and down the hill. Rose put the cup where it landed.

"Let's run the whole machine one more time," Terrance said.

Terrance was being bossy. But he was also being a good leader. He made sure everyone had a job.

This time we tested the whole machine. Terrance tipped over the first domino. We watched the last one hit the ball. It bounced and rolled and turned and went through our machine. At the end, the ball flew off the cliff and landed in the cup!

We all cheered and gave each other fist bumps. Just then, the lunch bell rang. We had finished right on time!

"Hey," I said, "we should all eat lunch

together."

Terrance frowned. "Let's take a vote. Put your hand up if you want to eat together."

Then he laughed and put his hand up. So did Jamal and Rose. Mr Aguilar laughed and said, "Let's all go. I'm hungry too!"

CHAPTER 10

CONGRATULATIONS AND RECOGNITIONS

On Friday morning, my class was colouring pictures of fractions. The intercom chime interrupted us. It was not the normal time for Friday announcements. Friday announcements were at the end of the day. My whole class stopped to listen.

"Good morning, everyone," said Ms Li. "Please excuse the interruption."

There was a long silence. I thought maybe Ms Li forgot what she was going to say. But then she started talking again.

"It has been a busy week in the STEM lab," the head said. "Ms Johnson's class worked on a project. They learned about energy and chain reactions. I visited the lab this morning. Everyone did an excellent job on their machines. I'm very impressed."

Rose and I smiled at each other.

"I would like to recognize Ms Johnson's class for a job well done," said Ms Li.

"Great!" yelled Terrance. "She's recognizing the whole class!"

"Shhh," said Ms Johnson. She wasn't annoyed, though. She was smiling.

"I tried each of your machines," Ms Li continued. "They *all* worked! Group two, congratulations for having the tallest machine."

The kids in group two smiled at each other.

I smiled too, but I was a little disappointed. Ms Li always did one congratulation and one recognition. That meant she was finished.

"I also have a very special congratulation and a thank you," said Ms Li. "This week, our guinea pig, Harry, went missing. Thanks to the excellent detective work of Azaleah Lane, Harry is safe and sound. He is back in his cage. Congratulations and thank you for putting so much *energy* into finding our furry friend."

My whole class clapped for me. I got a congratulation *and* a thank you.

"That's not all," said Ms Li.

"This is a *loooonnnnng* announcement." Terrance laughed.

Ms Li kept going. "I also happen to know that Azaleah was an excellent problem solver during the project. She should be recognized for her leadership."

My whole class cheered for me when Ms Li finished talking. And out of everyone,

Terrance cheered the loudest.

I couldn't believe it! I had been given congratulations *and* a thank you *and* recognitions! I wondered how Ms Li knew about our group's problem. I looked over at Ms Johnson. She winked at me.

Without permission, Terrance got up and walked over to me. Ms Li was still talking over the speaker. Ms Johnson opened her mouth, and I knew Terrance was about to get a reminder.

Before Ms Johnson could say anything, Terrance said, "Congratulations, Azaleah. You were a good problem solver. And I'm sorry I wasn't a good listener. I'll make sure everyone's vote counts next time."

Ms Johnson closed her mouth and smiled at Terrance.

I smiled at Terrance too. "Apology accepted."

"Yay, Azaleah!" yelled Rose.

Then the whole class yelled, "Yay, Azaleah!"

I was so proud I felt like I was growing. I couldn't wait to tell Mum and Dad.

"That is all," said Ms Li. "Thank you for listening to the extra announcements today. Have a great weekend!"

Oh, I will, I thought. *Because I just had the best day ever!*

PHOTO BY ALAN BRADLEY OF AFBPHOTOGRAPHY

ABOUT THE AUTHOR

Nikki Shannon Smith is from Oakland, California, USA, but she now lives in the Central Valley with her husband and two children. She has worked in elementary school education for more than 25 years, and writes everything from picture books to young adult novels. When she's not busy with family, work or writing, she loves to visit the sea. The first thing she packs in her suitcase is always a book.

PHOTO BY FRANCISCO SANTOYO

ABOUT THE ILLUSTRATOR

Gloria Félix was born and raised in Uruapan, a beautiful, small city in Michoacán, Mexico. Her home is one of her biggest inspirations when it comes to art. Her favourite things to do when she was little were drawing, watching cartoons and eating, which are still some of her favourite things to do. Gloria currently lives and paints in Los Angeles, California, USA.

GLOSSARY

chain reaction series of reactions that cause more reactions of the same kind

chemical reaction change that happens when two or more substances combine to form a new one

election process of choosing someone or deciding something by voting

energy ability to do work, such as moving things or giving heat or light

escape artist someone (such as an entertainer) who is good at escaping

monitor person who keeps track of a place or situation

nocturnal active at night and resting during the day

rascal mischievous person or animal

research study and learn about a subject

STEM abbreviation for science, technology, engineering and mathematics

vote make a choice

LET'S TALK

1. Azaleah asks her family what to do about Terrance. Mum suggests talking to the teacher. Dad suggests talking to Terrance. Nia suggests pretending to be a character to solve the problem. Tiana says to use her words. Which advice would you have taken? Why?
2. Think about a time when you had to solve a problem. What was it? Talk about how you came up with a solution to solve it.
3. Ms Li tells Mr Aguilar to close the STEM lab until Harry is found. Do you agree with Ms Li's decision? Talk about why or why not.
4. At the end of the story, Azaleah wonders how Ms Li knew about her group's problem. How do you think Ms Li found out? What clues from the story can you find? Talk about your ideas.

LET'S WRITE

1. Azaleah spends a lot of time trying to solve her Terrance problem. What if she had decided to write a letter to Terrance? What do you think it might say? Pretend you're Azaleah. Write a letter to Terrance to help solve the problem with the group.
2. Imagine you are Harry the guinea pig. Write a short story about your adventures while you were out of your cage. Include details from the book.
3. If your school was getting a new pet, what would you want it to be? Choose an animal, and then make a list of all the things it would need. You might have to do some research for this one!

MAKE A CHAIN-REACTION MACHINE!

Try making a fun chain-reaction machine that does a simple job. Some machines use a chain reaction to pour water. Others drop something into a cup, container or bucket. Some machines can even turn off a light!

You can make a machine just like Azaleah and her group did. You can build a machine that makes a ball land in a cup, or you can make it do something different.

What you need:

There are no rules for your machine, as long as you have permission from an adult. Here are some things you might use:

- blocks and other building materials
- boards
- cardboard
- cups
- dominoes (empty cereal boxes can be used like giant dominoes!)
- empty food cans
- kitchen towel rolls
- magnets
- paper
- pencils
- plastic containers
- rolls of tape
- small balls or marbles
- small weights
- string
- tin foil
- toilet paper rolls
- toy cars

What to do:

1. First, decide what you want your machine to do. (There are a lot of jobs a machine can do. It can even water a plant or pop a balloon!)
2. Find a good place to create your machine. You might need to leave it up for a few days, so make sure it won't be in the way.
3. Gather materials for your machine.
4. Sketch a picture of your plan. (It's okay if you change materials or your plan while you're building your machine.)
5. Build your machine one part at a time and test it. If one part doesn't work, make changes.
6. After you get your machine completed, test it out.
7. Keep adjusting your machine until it works exactly the way you want it to!

FUN FACT: Did you know, people with STEM jobs use trial and error all the time? That's what experiments are. You try something to see if it works. If it doesn't, you keep trying until you get it right. It is how we get new inventions and new medicines! It's okay if your machine doesn't work the first time. Try something, and if it doesn't work, see how you can fix it.

TIP: If you are having a really hard time thinking of ideas, ask an adult if you can use the internet. You'll find lots of videos about chain-reaction machines online.

AZALEAH LANE
FINDS MYSTERY AND ADVENTURE AROUND EVERY CORNER.
CHECK OUT THE FIRST BOOK IN THE SERIES!
THE AMAZING LIFE OF AZALEAH LANE